THE KING AND HIS SON

Christopher Felder

Tatyana Takushevich, Illustrator

Jessica Ayers, Copy Editor

gatekeeper press™
Columbus, OH

The King and His Son

Published by Gatekeeper Press
2167 Stringtown Rd, Suite 109
Columbus, OH 43123-2989
www.GatekeeperPress.com

ISBN (hardcover): 9781662911361

One day Samuel came home from school upset because he'd been picked on by other kids. His father asked what was wrong, but Samuel didn't answer.

He went to his room and stayed there for a long time. When his mother knocked on the door and came in, she asked Samuel what was wrong. Again, he said nothing and asked to be left alone. His mother agreed and left his room

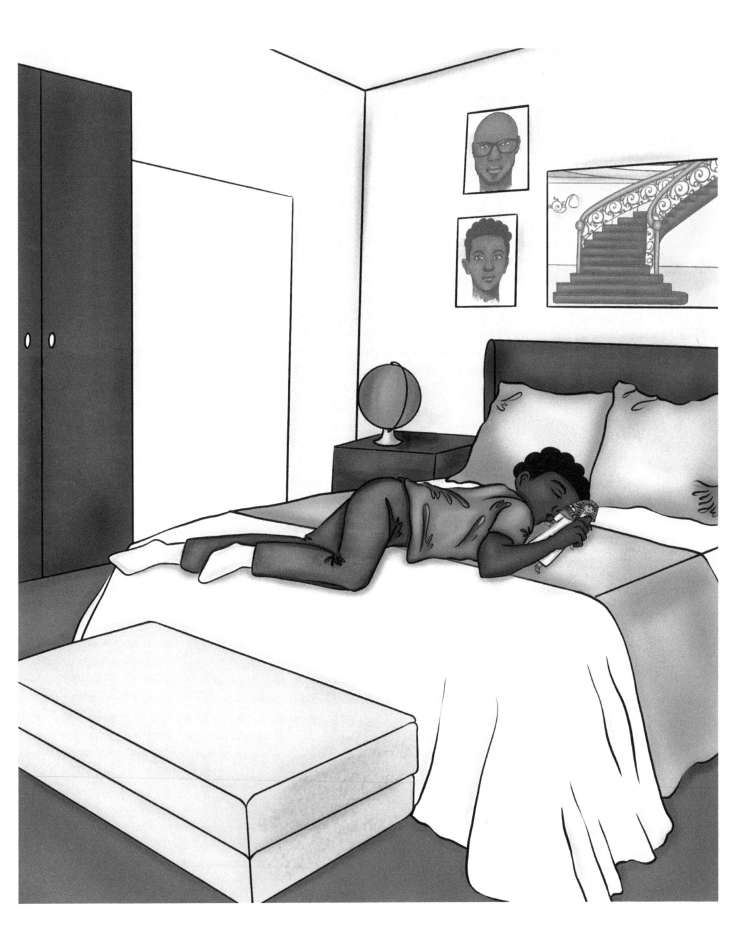

Samuel began to cry as he held the doll of a king his father had given him.
Not long after, he fell asleep.

When Samuel awoke, he was no longer in his room. He was in a big bed, even bigger than his parents' bed. Out the window, there was nothing but hills of green trees covered by rays of the sun.

Samuel walked out of the room and looked down a large hallway filled with guards and a long rug that led to a staircase.

"Prince Samuel, your father awaits you downstairs," said one of the guards.
"Prince?" Samuel questioned.
"Come, sir, there is much to discuss," replied the guard. Still in his school
clothes, Samuel nervously walked down the hallway
and the massive flight of stairs.

At the bottom of the stairs, Samuel saw an incredible sight. His father sat on a throne while his mother stood, hand extended towards her son.

"Mom? Dad?" Samuel was confused and amazed at how powerful his parents looked. He walked towards them, staring in amazement. His mother smiled, but his father stared back with a stern face, saying nothing.

"Mom, where are we?" asked Samuel.

"My child, we are home," his mother answered. "Your father wishes to speak with you on a pressing matter." Samuel looked at his father, who kept his eyes fixed on his son.

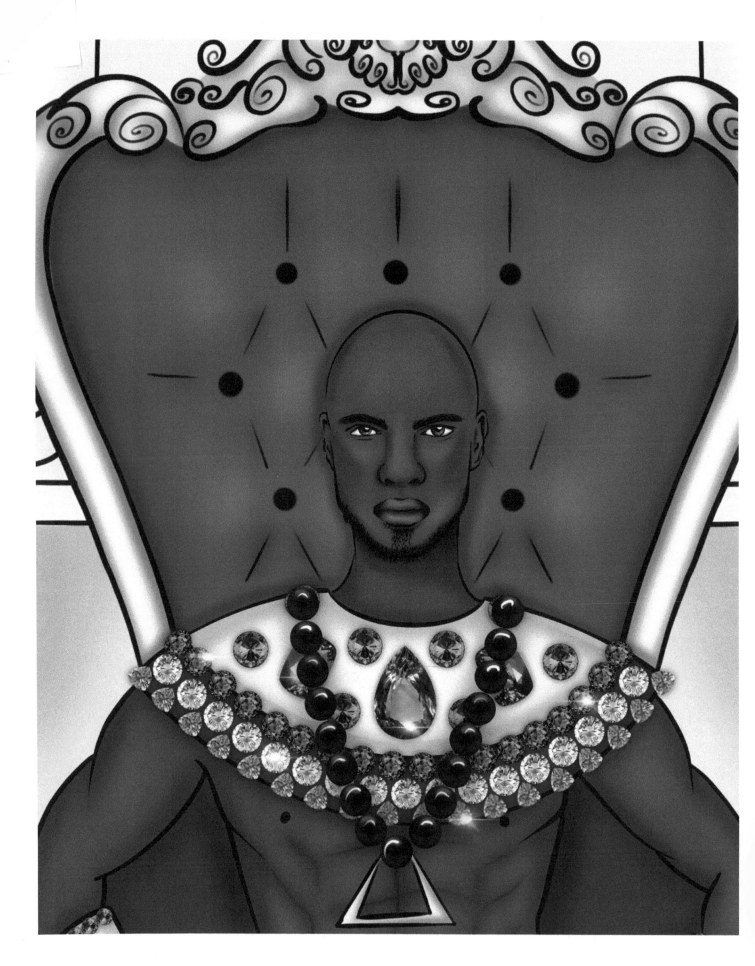

"My son, what is your last name?" asked his father.

"My last name?" replied Samuel.

"Yes. What is your last name?" his father asked again.

"I have the same last name as you, Dad," Samuel answered timidly.

His father's eyes didn't move or even blink; he said nothing.

"Why are you asking me about my last name?"

"Do you know why you are a prince?" Samuel's father asked.
"I didn't know I was a prince, Dad. I just thought I was your son,"
replied Samuel.

"You are my son. You are the son of a king, and because you are the son of a king, that makes you a prince. Do you understand?"

"When did you become a king, Dad?" asked Samuel.

"I became a king when I grew up to be a man. But I was once a prince too. As a prince, you must have confidence and believe you are a prince. Others who think less of you will try to treat you like you are meaningless. You must remember you are a prince, and you deserve respect," Samuel's father said.

"What is respect, Dad?" asked Samuel.

His father now rose from his throne and walked towards his son. As the King approached, he laid his hand upon Samuel's shoulder.

"My son, respect is simply acknowledging the importance of a person, whether it is us, the guards, or people outside the castle."

Samuel looked down at his feet.

"I don't feel like people respect me father," he said, feeling his eyes watering again. The King took his hand and slowly lifted his son's head.
"Son, people will only respect you when you respect yourself. You can never bow your head in shame. You must understand and love who you are. Do you love me and your mother?" asked the King.
"Yes, sir," replied Samuel.

"Do you love yourself?" asked the King.

"How do I love myself?" asked Samuel, confused.

"You love yourself by believing in yourself the way you believe in us," the King answered, guiding his son back towards the stairs. "As a boy, you must understand that you cannot wait to believe in yourself at an older age—the time must start now. Everyone will think of you how they want to. That doesn't matter."

"It doesn't?" Samuel asked quizzically.

"Of course not! I am a king, not because others believed in who I am but because I believed in myself. Do you understand?" the King asked, stopping suddenly. They arrived back at Samuel's room. "You must believe in and respect yourself before you can ask anyone else to do the same. Will you do this, my son?" the King asked, leaning over and looking straight into his son's eyes. Samuel straightened his back, standing tall.

"I will, Father," answered Samuel, beaming with confidence.

"Good, now you must wake up."

Samuel suddenly awoke in his room. He had been dreaming but still felt the powerful words of the King. There was a knock on the door, and Samuel's father opened it and entered.

"Is everything okay, son?" his father asked.

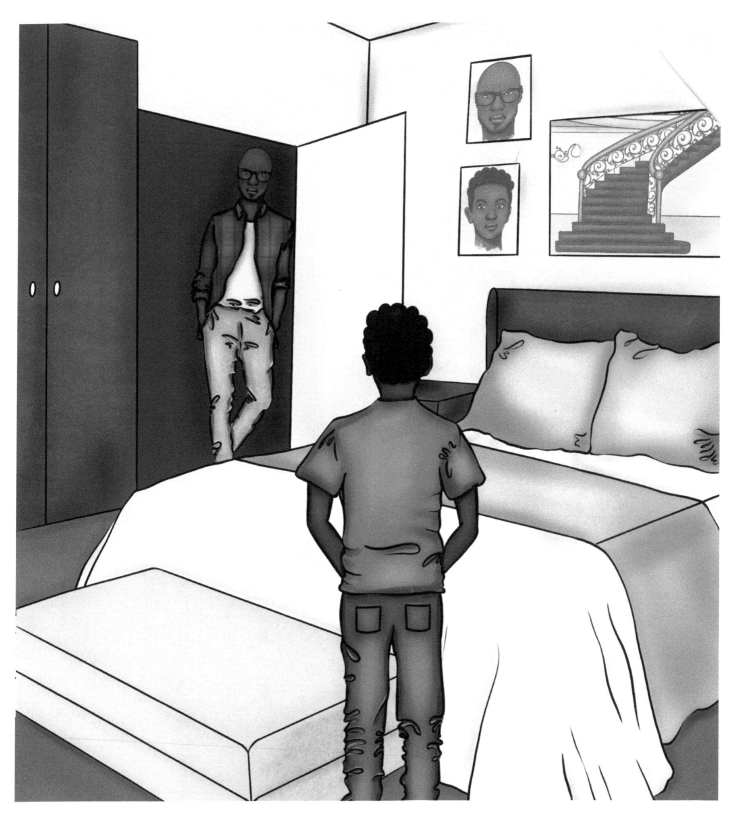

"Yeah, it's just these kids at my school were picking on me, and I was upset."

"Did you tell your teacher?" his father asked, concerned.

"I did, but it still made me feel bad. I don't see why those kids made fun of me in the first place." Samuel's father looked at his son from above his glasses.

"Let me ask you something, son. What is your last name?"

The End.